TO: ADDISON

LOVE - GG
12/22

CAN YOU TEACH ME?

Copyright © Harleigh M. Clark. 2022.
All Rights Reserved.
ISBN: 978-7327858-4-7
Published in the United States
by Positivity Lady Press
Robbinston, ME 04671

POSITIVITY LADY PRESS

For all inquiries, please contact us at: support@positivityladypress.com

Thank you to everyone who makes time
to teach kids how to do new things.

Ask an adult to help you and try making the cookies
that Kinsleigh, London, and Lilliana baked.

FAVORITE CHOCOLATE CHIP COOKIES

- 1 cup salted butter, softened
- 1 ¼ cup light brown sugar, firmly packed
- 2 tsp pure vanilla extract
- 2 large eggs
- 2 ¼ cups all-purpose flour, packed
- 1/2 tsp baking soda
- 1 tsp salt
- 16 oz choc chips (or candy-coated chocolate pieces)

INSTRUCTIONS

Preheat oven to 375 degrees F. Line a baking pan
with parchment paper and set aside.
In a separate bowl mix flour, baking soda, and salt.
Set aside.
Cream together butter and brown sugar until combined.
Beat in eggs and vanilla until fluffy.
Mix in the dry ingredients until combined.
Add chocolate chips and mix well.
Drop by teaspoon onto your prepared cookie sheets.
Bake in preheated oven for approximately 8-10 minutes.
Take them out when the edges are just turning brown.
Let them sit on the baking pan for 2 minutes
before removing to cooling rack.

**Makes about 60 cookies
(depending on how big you decide to make them.)**

This is author Harleigh's favorite chocolate chip cookie recipe.
It's one her Great Nana used and passed down to her.

ABOUT THE AUTHOR

HARLEIGH CLARK IS A 10-YEAR OLD WHO LOVES CHEERLEADING, BAKING COOKIES AND BRAIDING HAIR... ESPECIALLY AT SLEEPOVERS. SHE LIVES IN MAINE WITH HER MOM, DAD, AND LITTLE BROTHER ALONG WITH THEIR KITTY, MITTENS AND PUPPY, TUCKER.

ABOUT THE ILLUSTRATOR

SVETLANA LAU IS A CHILDREN'S BOOK
ILLUSTRATOR WHO COLLECTS VINYL RECORDS
AND BOOKS, VISITS MUSEUMS, LIKES TO TRAVEL,
AND IS MAMA TO A FOUR-YEAR-OLD BOY.

Made in the USA
Middletown, DE
06 December 2022

17247463R00020